The Snow Dragon

In memory of Ronald,
our original Snow Dragon
C.F. and V.F.

For Jonathan
with love
C.F.

The Snow Dragon

Vivian French

Illustrated by Chris Fisher

Picture Corgi Books

THE·FIRST HAPPENING

 N THE BEGINNING WAS A WORLD, AND IT WAS DIVIDED INTO TWO HALVES. THE SOUTHERN HALF WAS BURNING HOT AND RULED BY FEROCIOUS FIRE DRAGONS, BUT IN THE COLD AND ICY NORTH LIVED THE PEACE-LOVING SNOW DRAGONS.

WHERE NORTH AND SOUTH CAME TOGETHER THERE WAS A LONG NARROW LAND OF WATER AND GREEN HILLS WHERE TALL TREES AND LEAFY PLANTS GREW, AND IN THIS LAND LIVED THE TWOLEGS.

THE TWOLEGS POTTERED ABOUT HAPPILY FOR MANY YEARS TENDING THE EARTH AND GROWING FRUIT AND FLOWERS, AND THE DRAGONS TOOK NO NOTICE OF THEM.

BUT THEN CAME A HAPPENING THAT CHANGED EVERYTHING.

AT THE TIME OF THE MAKING OF THE WORLD A BOOK WAS WRITTEN, A BOOK SO
SPECIAL THAT IT WAS ALWAYS KNOWN SIMPLY AS BOOK.

SOMETIMES BOOK WAS A HANDBOOK OF INSTRUCTIONS ON HOW THE WORLD
WORKED, AND THE DRAGONS FOUND IT VERY USEFUL. AT OTHER TIMES BOOK WAS
ABLE (IF IT FELT LIKE IT) TO TELL THE FUTURE.
IT WAS THIS THAT CAUSED THE HAPPENING.

The Happening began when the Most Royal of Fire Dragons himself called for Book.

"Book," he rumbled, "tell me if one day I will be Lord of all the world... South and North together!"

Book sniggered, and showed a picture of a scurrying beetle.

The Most Royal of Fire Dragons grew angry. "Answer me, Book!" he thundered, and his burning breath singed Book's pages brown.

Book glared at the Fire Dragon. "Fire worm!" it hissed. "READ! And see the future!" and it opened its pages wide.

BEHOLD! THE TIME IS COMING WHEN FIRE DRAGONS

WILL BE NO MORE...

The Fire Dragon stared, and stared again.

"How can this be true?" he snarled. "Who could ever defeat ME?"

Book turned another page.

A TWOLEG.

"A Twoleg!" sneered Book. "Tee hee! Tee hee! The Fire Dragons will be defeated by a Twoleg!"

The Most Royal of Fire Dragons roared such a terrible blast of flame that the skies turned to burning crimson, and he hurled Book away into the darkness of the swirling smoke and ashes.

From that moment on life became a misery for all Twolegs. The Fire Dragons hunted them down and blackened their plants and scorched the earth around them. The Twolegs took to living underground in dark caves and dusty scratched-out tunnels.

As time went on the Fire Dragons
flew further and further North
spreading heat and dryness. The
peace-loving Snow Dragons were driven
further and further back behind huge mountains
of snow and ice – until it was thought that there
were no Snow Dragons left alive.

BUT THEN CAME

THE SECOND HAPPENING.

THE SECOND HAPPENING

There were many orphans among the Twolegs.

One such orphan was Little Tuft. He lived with the very oldest Twoleg who told him wonderful stories about life as it had been before the Happening: stories of the shining sun, and green plants, and the rush and splash of the streams and rivers. Little Tuft listened spellbound. His favourite story was of the magical Snow Dragons who loved peace, and who never went to war.

"Why can't we go and find one?" Little Tuft asked, but the oldest Twoleg was stone deaf, and only smiled and nodded.

Little Tuft stopped asking questions, but as soon as he grew tall enough to open the huge wooden door that protected the Twolegs from the world outside he crept out. He wanted to see for himself what was going on.

Outside the caves Little Tuft stared all around. The earth was charred and burnt and blackened, but the sky was clear and blue. After his years in the gloom of the tunnels Little Tuft could not believe the lightness and brightness. He took a deep breath, and began to walk. Somewhere there was a way to bring back the magic green land that the oldest Twolegs told such wonderful stories about. There had to be a way – and he, Little Tuft, was going to find it, even if –

WHEEEEEEEEEEEEEEEEEEeeeeeeeeeeeeeeeeeeeeeeeee!!!!!!!
Little Tuft found himself slipping and sliding down a deep dark chasm between two rocks. Down and down he went, gasping and grabbing at the crumbling earth until –

THUMP!!!!!!
– he landed at the bottom.

"Excuse ME," said a rusty dusty voice, "but would you mind NOT treading all over me with your grubby little feet?"

Little Tuft had found Book.

Little Tuft scrabbled and struggled and heaved and hauled himself and Book back up to the sunlight. There he sat down to rest, and Book slyly fluttered his pages open.

Little Tuft gasped.
"I can see a Snow Dragon!" he whispered, and he rubbed his eyes. "It almost looks as if it's alive!"
"Ahem," said Book. "Pay attention! This is the Most Royal Snow Dragon, asleep in her Ice Palace."

"But is it true? Is she alive?" asked Little Tuft, breathless in his excitement.
"Of COURSE she's alive, you foolish Twoleg!" snapped Book.
Little Tuft jumped up. "Then," he said, "we must find her!"
So Little Tuft set off to find the Snow Dragon. Book went with him.

Dark Seas

Land of the Snowdragon

Desert

Forest

Swamp

Fire Dragons

Sometimes Book showed Little Tuft the right roads, and sometimes it led him into bogs and quick sands and waterless deserts.

As they tramped along, Book warned Little Tuft when a Fire Dragon was near... but sometimes it forgot, and Little Tuft had to scramble into hiding while Book sniggered loudly.

And as they travelled further and further North they saw fewer and fewer Fire Dragons, until one day they saw none at all...

At last they began to trudge across snow and ice, and the air was full of frost and silver flakes. Little Tuft's footprints stretched behind them; there was no other mark on the wastes of frozen white.

The gates to the Ice Palace were encrusted with icicles, but Little Tuft was small enough to slide between the bars. Book mumbled and grumbled as Little Tuft tugged it after him.

The Most Royal of Snow Dragons was asleep. Silence hung in the air around her.

Little Tuft held his breath, and stood still in the doorway.

"Well?" said Book, and flapped its pages. "Well? I thought this was what we came all this miserable way to see!"

"Ssh!" Little Tuft whispered, but the Snow Dragon was stirring.

Slowly she stretched herself. Longer and longer and longer she grew. Little Tuft stared at her. He couldn't think of anything to say.

"Get on with it!" hissed Book.

The Snow Dragon turned her head and gazed at them. "Book?" she asked. "Is it you? And a Twoleg?"

Little Tuft began to stutter. "P-p-p-p p-p-p please – I need your help."

"Twoleg!" the Most Royal of Snow Dragons reared up, and Little Tuft trembled. "Listen! It was written in Book that a Twoleg would bring defeat to the Fire Dragons... and there was war... a terrible, terrible war."

The Snow Dragon stopped, her eyes full of cold tears. "Of all the Snow Dragons, only I am left. Why should I help you, Twoleg? Fight the Fire Dragons yourself."

Little Tuft was blue with cold, but he took a deep breath. "Oh, Your Majesty – you don't understand. The Twolegs don't want to fight. All they want is a little land where they can live in peace. Look at us! Book will show you!"

Book stayed firmly closed.

"Oh..." Little Tuft's voice began to shake. "Perhaps – perhaps it doesn't know—"

"RUBBISH!" Book strutted forward. "I know EVERYTHING!"

It opened its pages wide, and the Snow Dragon saw the burnt and wasted world. A page turned, and a Twoleg baby cried and cried in a dark and murky cavern. Another page, and Little Tuft was struggling across a blackened desert, bent down under Book.

The Snow Dragon looked down at Little Tuft. "Yes," she said, and her voice was gentle. "The Twolegs are very small and weak. But they are still brave enough to walk through fire to ask for help for one another... so, yes. I will help you."

The steady beat of the Snow Dragon's wings lulled Little Tuft into a half sleep. He was certain that now everything would be made right. The Most Royal of Snow Dragons would know what to do.

Little Tuft shut his eyes and leant back against the mighty silver wing. "Book," he said happily, "it'll soon be a Happy Ever After ending."

Book made a snarling noise. "I HATE happy ever afters. That's no sort of story for a Book like me!" It began to open and close its covers angrily.

"Book!" Little Tuft sat up. "What are you doing?"

"I'm going to change the ending, that's what!" Book looked at Little Tuft and sneered. "Watch... and see what you will see! Tee hee! Tee hee! Tee hee..."

And Book leapt off the Snow Dragon's back and half flew, half floated into the grey clouds below.

"OH! OH!" Little Tuft cried out. "Oh, Snow Dragon! What will happen?"

The Snow Dragon heaved a deep and painful sigh. "The Fire Dragons will know that we are coming."

Little Tuft hung on tightly to the Snow Dragon's scaly neck. "But we can still save the world?"

"Look, Little Tuft," said the Snow Dragon, and Little Tuft looked far ahead.

A huge volcano was belching red and yellow flames high into the sky, and Fire Dragons soared in and out of the glittering sparks that showered from its glowing crater. Little Tuft stared in horror as clouds of thick black smoke swirled into words:

MOST ROYAL OF
FIRE DRAGONS
KING OF ALL
THE WORLD

"Book has arrived," said the Snow Dragon.

Little Tuft began to cry. "What can we do?" he sobbed.

The Snow Dragon did not answer. She began to circle, and with a scraping of scales against the rocks landed on a bare mountain.

"Little Tuft," she said. "I must leave you here."

"NO!" said Little Tuft. "PLEASE, most wonderful Snow Dragon – please don't go home! I didn't mean to cry – but we can't just give up! PLEASE."

The Snow Dragon picked Little Tuft off her back and dropped him gently onto the ground. "Dear Little Tuft," she said. "You've made your journey. It is my turn now." She kissed him with a cold icy kiss, and flew up and up and away.

Little Tuft stood and watched as she circled once above him, and then his eyes opened wide. The Snow Dragon was not flying back to the North. She was flying directly towards the volcano.

If the last of the smoke letters had not been covering the sky the Fire Dragons might have seen the Snow Dragon in time to stop her. As it was they were too late. She came hurtling down into the very heart of the fire, and as she dived the fire and smoke changed to hissing fountains of boiling steam that shot high in the air – and cooled into weird and wonderful spikes and turrets and pinnacles of ice. Fire Dragons raged and roared and rampaged in the smoke and the steam, but one by one they melted away into cinders that glowed for one last moment and then went out. PH'T T T T T

Then came the snow. Little Tuft, sitting on his mountain, saw heavy clouds rolling out of the crater and covering the world as far as he could see. Great white flakes softly, gently fell and went on falling. Little Tuft shivered and huddled under the rocks for shelter. He went on watching for the Snow Dragon until he was frozen with cold, but she never came back.

The snow lay crisp and white in hills and hollows for grey day after grey day. Little Tuft scraped and scratched himself a little cave, and waited.

Then, one morning, the sun came leaping up into the sky – and the snow began to melt. Beneath the snow the earth was green – and the sky above was brilliant blue. Drifts of snow heaved and hollowed and burst open, and Twolegs came creeping and scrambling out into the light. They held up their arms to the sun, and they shouted and laughed and cried with joy.

Little Tuft began to jump down the rocks, but halfway he suddenly stopped. There were snow-white clouds along the horizon – and for a second he thought he had caught a glimpse of the Snow Dragon lying in among them.

Little Tuft rubbed his eyes. Was it really the Snow Dragon? Or a cloud? He shook his head. He would never know for certain, but he waved – just in case.

hen he ran on to join the other Twolegs to be hugged
and kissed – and to argue about who should be the
first to dig the earth and sow the seeds.

AND BOOK? WHO KNOWS. BUT FOR THE MOMENT –

THE END

THE SNOW DRAGON
A PICTURE CORGI BOOK : 978 0 552 54595 2

First published in Great Britain by Doubleday, a division of
Random House Children's Books

PRINTING HISTORY
Doubleday edition published 1999
Picture Corgi edition published 2000

12 13 14 15 16 17 18 19 20

Picture Corgi Books are published by Random House Children's Books,
61-63 Uxbridge Road, London W5 5SA,
a division of The Random House Group Ltd

Addresses for companies within The Random House Group Limited can be found
at: www.randomhouse.co.uk/offices.htm

Printed in Singapore

www.**kidsatrandomhouse**.co.uk